Carol Roth
The Little School Bus
Illustrated by Pamela Paparone

A CHESHIRE STUDIO BOOK

North
South

For my darling grandsons Jake and Ethan.
With all my love —C.R.

For Richard —P.P.

Text copyright © 2002 by Carol Roth
Illustrations copyright © 2002 by Pamela Paparone
All rights reserved. No part of this book may be reproduced or utilized
in any form or by any means, electronic or mechanical, including photocopying,
recording, or any information storage and retrieval system, without
permission in writing from the publisher.

A CHESHIRE STUDIO BOOK
First published in the United States, Great Britain, Canada,
Australia, and New Zealand in 2002 by NorthSouth Books,
an imprint of NordSüd Verlag AG, CH-8005, Zürich, Switzerland.
Distributed in the United States by NorthSouth Books Inc., New York.
Library of Congress Cataloging-in-Publication Data is available.
The CIP catalogue record for this book is available from The British Library.
For more information about our books, and the authors and artists
who create them, visit our web site: www.northsouth.com

ISBN 0-7358-1646-8 (trade edition)
1 3 5 7 9 HC 10 8 6 4 2
ISBN 0-7358-1647-6 (library edition)
1 3 5 7 9 LE 10 8 6 4 2
ISBN: 978-0-7358-1905-4 (paperback edition)
5 7 9 PB 10 8 6
Printed in China by Leo paper Products Ltd.,
Kowloon Bay, Hong Kong, July 2014.

Here comes the school bus,
beep, beep, beep!
Step right up and take a seat,
and ride the bus to school, to school,
and ride the bus to school.

The first one on is a little goat
wearing his new winter coat,
riding the bus to school, to school,
riding the bus to school.

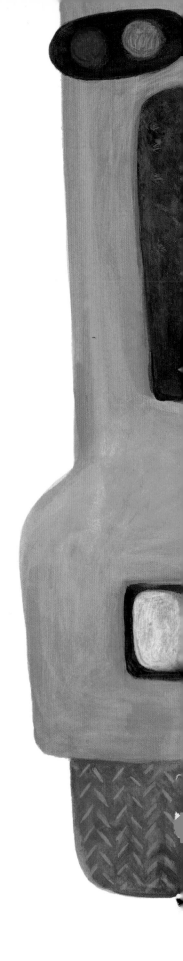

The second one on is a pretty pig
and on her head is a curly wig.
A pig in a wig,
a goat in his coat,
riding the bus to school, to school,
riding the bus to school.

The third one on is a sly, sly fox.
He has no shoes, but he's wearing socks.
A fox with socks,

a pig in a wig,
a goat in his coat,
riding the bus to school, to school,
riding the bus to school.

The fourth one on is a fuzzy chick.
She hops on the bus so quick, quick, quick.

A quick, quick chick,
a fox with socks,
a pig in a wig,
a goat in his coat,

riding the bus to school, to school,
riding the bus to school.

The fifth one on is a hairy bear.
His messy hair is everywhere.
A hairy bear,

a quick, quick chick,
a fox with socks,
a pig in a wig,
a goat in his coat,

riding the bus to school, to school,

riding the bus to school.

The sixth one on is a wiggly worm.
He can't sit still, so he starts to squirm.
A squirmy worm,
a hairy bear,

a quick, quick chick,
a fox with socks,
a pig in a wig,
a goat in his coat,

riding the bus to school, to school,

riding the bus to school.

The last one on is a sleepy sheep.
She curls right up and falls asleep.
A sleepy sheep,
a squirmy worm,

a hairy bear,
a quick, quick chick,
a fox with socks,
a pig in a wig,
a goat in his coat,

riding the bus to school, to school,
riding the bus to school.

During school they learn and play,

while the little bus sits and waits all day.

And when the school day finally ends,

the little bus starts right up again.

There goes the school bus,
beep, beep, beep!
Everybody's in their seat:
a sleepy sheep,

a squirmy worm,
a hairy bear,
a quick, quick chick,
a fox with socks,
a pig in a wig,
a goat in his coat,

riding home from school, from school,
riding home from school.